WARNING

This book contains sexually explicit scenes and adult language. It may be considered offensive to some readers. This book is for sale to adults ONLY.

* * * * * * * * * * * * * * * * *

Please store your files wisely where they cannot be accessed by underage readers.

DISCLAIMER

ISBN-13: 978-1987863253
ISBN-10: 1987863259

Other Books by Darla Dunbar:

<u>The Romeo Alpha BBW Paranormal Shifter Romance Series</u>

Amanda Walker thinks that she has a normal and boring life. That is until after her 24th birthday. Everything changes when she meets the man who says he was supposed to be her husband. Denying everything the man says, she fights him every step of the way. But after he kidnaps her, Amanda discovers that there are some things about her family that her parents kept a secret all these years. Among the history of the family she learns secrets she thought only happened in story books. Can Amanda tell the difference between truth and lies or is she this mysterious woman that holds the key to a legacy?

<u>Romeo Alpha Blood Lines Romance Series</u>

Twenty-four years have passed in relative peace for Amanda and Romeo. They've raised five children into adulthood and are thoroughly enjoying their lives as the Alpha King and Queen of the werewolves. At twenty-four, Sarina is just stepping into her powers and will be ripe for mating when her birthday comes in two weeks. What no one knows is the danger that lurks just outside their tight knit community. Romeo has made peace with the other clans and has enjoyed that peace, but it will all come crashing down around him when his oldest daughter comes of age to take a mate.

The Alpha Feud BBW Paranormal Shifter Romance Series

Eliza's life consisted of reporting on boring, crowd-pleasing events, like their country livestock fair. With the arrival of two handsome brothers, the lives of Eliza and her best friend, Melissa, are shaken to the core. For Eliza, the arrival of this new man becomes a test of her relationship with her current boyfriend, who she's been happily living with for over six years. Does Hayden, a complete stranger, really wield the power to make Eliza reconsider her relationship with Andrew?

The Alpha Packed BBW Paranormal Shifter Romance Series

Darlene has led a quiet life since suffering through a terrible break-up. She wants nothing more than to spend her time in front of the TV, away from any sort of trouble. But all that goes down the drain when handsome, rugged and rough Idris comes into her life. He is a werewolf on the lookout for his missing pack leader. Darlene quickly finds herself pulled towards this mysterious man and at the same time finds herself falling deeper and deeper into the world of the supernatural.

The Daemon Paranormal Romance Chronicles

The daemon infighting can only be stopped when a strong leader emerges to calm the different factions. Juno appears to be at the heart of the conflict. Things become complicated when Phoebe and Supay try to negotiate with the siren, Juno. The love triangle among Phoebe, Supay and Apollo become tense when Juno's meddling threatens to destroy any romance that develops.

<u>The Mind Talker Paranormal Romance Series</u>

Ananda finds herself on the run and she's not alone. With help from Jared, a stranger that she just met, the two evade capture by an organization that is intent on hunting her kind. Ananda and Jared are able to read minds. When an unfortunate incident happened involving a disturbed individual that resulted in the death of his schoolmates, the secret organization decided to take action.

Get the latest update on new releases from the author at:

https://darladunbar.com/newsletter/

This book is Part Five of "<u>The Leather Satchel</u> <u>Paranormal Romance Series</u>"

Book 1 - Valtina's Redemption

Valtina is stuck in Middle World, unable to pass on to The Afterlife. In order to redeem herself from past deeds done, she must help bring romance back into the world and stop The Dark Side from destroying love in its entirety. Following orders issued by Ladaya and armed with a leather satchel filled with the appropriate tools and weapons, Valtina must bring romance back into the lives of Samantha and Joshua, thereby saving their marriage.

Book 2 - Unfaithful

Amy and Matt's relationship was never meant to be. The evil forces at work are bent on eliminating love on Earth. Couples are being mismatched in order to create chaos. It is Valtina's mission the help Amy find her soul mate and repair the damage that is being caused by the dark forces.

Book 3 - Evil Lust

Henry and Claire are meant to be together. But a succubus has taken over Henry's actions. Under her spell, Henry has succumbed to lusting after Charlotte, the human form that the succubus has assumed. If Claire were to find out, then their marriage will be ruined beyond repair. It is up to Valtina to break the succubus' spell and clear Henry's memory of any guilt that would haunt his love for Claire forever.

Book 4 - Salvaged Soul Mates

The Dark Side is winning. A Mystic has organized the evil monsters to steal every soul on Earth and leave it loveless. It is up to Valtina to do her part to save the human race. Sent by Ladaya back to Earth, Valtina's job is to unite a mismatched couple with their true soul-mates. Sebastian and Claudia were not meant to be married to each other. But a trickster was involved in encouraging the mismatch. Searching through her leather satchel, Valtina found the tools needed to do the job.

Book 5 - Fury of Lust

Valtina's missions are becoming more dangerous and will need the protection of a warrior and emere while out on duty. This time she needs to rid Rachel of a fury and free Sean of his demons. Rachel and Sean are meant to be true lovers but they have been prevented from meeting each other. Valtina must use the arsenal in her leather satchel to ensure that true love follows its course when Rachel and Sean finally meet.

Book 6 - True Lovers

Middle World has been invaded by the wraiths. While the Generals battle the monsters to protect Middle World, Valtina must continue her missions to save love on Earth. The evil forces have brain-washed Penelope and Davis into thinking that their attraction for each other is wrong. Valtina's mission is to clear the way for the couple to see that they were meant for each other and to let true love runs its fateful course.

The Leather Satchel Paranormal Romance Series

Fury of Lust

Book Five

By Darla Dunbar

Copyright Revelry Publishing 2015

Table of Contents

Chapter One

"**VALTINA, I'M** so sorry it took me so long to get back. My superior summoned us all to explain the new protocol. I'm afraid our forces continue to be overwhelmed by the evil armies. Two dozen spirits failed to report back after their assignments this week. Undoubtedly they've been captured by wraiths." Ladaya spoke quickly… time was not a luxury she had, given the current circumstances. She continued, "We can no longer afford to risk sending you out on your own. From now on, you will be accompanied on all of your missions by two protectors… a warrior and an emere. I've assigned Demetri as your warrior… I know you've worked well together in the past. Fatima will be your emere. She will meet you at your destination."

Valtina finally spoke. "Ladaya, what is an emere? I don't think I've ever heard you mention one before."

"I'm sorry, child. Of course you wouldn't know about emeres. The emeres are the purest form of spirits. They left the mortal world when they were infants, so their souls were never tarnished. Fatima and the other emeres have powers far more potent than even my own. And they can move freely between The Afterlife and Earth. They cannot come to Middle World, but Fatima will be able to send you home after your mission, or if you're in imminent danger. I cannot stress this enough,

Valtina. You must stay vigilant and be on constant guard against danger."

Valtina was saddened by Ladaya's appearance. Gone was the carefree, wise woman who had guided her on her journey to The Afterlife. Now, Ladaya stood before her in torn robes, her hair undone and wild, and her kind eyes filled with despair. When Valtina had agreed to join the spirit army to fight against the evil forces, she'd imagined that she would receive her final reward after one or two missions. As the weeks went on, however, Valtina realized that she may never reach The Afterlife. Her destiny, it seemed, was to valiantly fight a losing battle.

"Ladaya, what can I expect to run into, besides the tricksters, succubi, and wraiths? I want to be prepared!"

"Valtina, I don't know how many kinds of monsters are now working against us. Morgonda seems to have rallied every creature that's ever been imagined. Our sources tell us that she's breeding them, combining wraith and lampades, demons and nymphs… she's designing her own unique army. I've heard she's even recruited scorned demigods to fight against us."

Valtina gasped. "Demigods? She's turning everything against us, isn't she?"

"She's doing her best to," Ladaya agreed, "but we must not be discouraged. And we must keep fighting. Are you ready for your next assignment?" Valtina responded by nodding. "I'm afraid this one may be your most challenging mission yet. You'll have Demetri and Fatima, of course, but I daresay their powers won't be much help for most of this. They're mainly along for your protection," said Ladaya.

"Ladaya, I know you've insisted on protecting me in the past, but don't Demetri and Fatima have better things to do than shadow me while I fix people's love lives? Surely they could be of more use somewhere else! I can protect myself!" Valtina insisted defiantly. It seemed to her that having two spirit babysitters was overkill. Valtina wanted to end the war as quickly as possible, so she could be reunited with her soul-mate in The Afterlife. If Demetri and Fatima worked their own assignments, they could defeat three evil situations in the time it would take them to defeat one together.

"Valtina, we are *not* arguing about this again," Ladaya answered firmly. "You may not understand your own importance, but the rest of us do. You are the culmination of every type of love that exists. *You* hold within you everything Morgonda and her armies are trying to defeat. We have other loving souls fighting for us, of course, but *you* are the most powerful. There is nothing more important than keeping you safe, and helping you to bring love back to the souls on Earth. *You* are our best chance of ridding the world from evil once and for all, Valtina!"

"Now," Ladaya continued, "your next mission. As I was saying, I'm afraid this will be your most difficult assignment yet. Rachel and Sean were supposed to meet in college and fall in love. They should have been married for six years now, but Morgonda's forces interfered. Rachel was possessed by a fury, and has been leading a dangerous, promiscuous, loveless life ever since. True love is the only power strong enough to expel a fury, so Sean has been well guarded, to ensure that the two never meet. Demons watch him day and night… study them and observe their shift schedule. You'll have to free Sean before you can help Rachel. This is a complicated case, Valtina, and we can't afford for you to become distracted like last time," Ladaya chided. Valtina blushed. During her last mission, she'd wasted nearly 14 hours daydreaming about her lives with her soul-mate. She opened her mouth to offer reassurance, but she was interrupted.

"Don't worry, Ladaya. I'll keep Valtina on task," Demetri smiled as he approached Valtina from behind.

"Ah, Demetri! I take it your General has described the mission to you?" Ladaya asked.

"Sure. Valtina's task is to defeat a demon, or maybe a few demons, expel a fury, and introduce soul-mates who've never met. I'll keep her on task and keep her safe. The emere will meet us at the destination. That's the gist of it, right?" Demetri asked casually, as if this kind of mission, this battle, was nothing of consequence. Valtina wondered who he'd been in his mortal lives, but was hesitant to ask.

"Yes Demetri, that's the gist of it," Ladaya said, sighing. "I look forward to hearing your report. Stay safe, and work quickly," she said softly, as the white mist appeared to transport Ladaya to The Afterlife and deliver Valtina and Demetri to Rachel's apartment.

Chapter Two

"Hello. I've been expecting you." A low, soft voice greeted Valtina and Demetri. Valtina turned to find the glowing, pearl white face of Fatima.

"It's nice to meet you. I'm Valtina."

"Yes. And you are Demetri," Fatima turned from Valtina to the warrior. "I'm sorry to meet you under these circumstances. I'm afraid this situation is dire. I arrived an hour ago, and I've been unable to enter Rachel's bedroom. That can only mean that there are things taking place within those walls that are so depraved, my soul cannot be exposed to them."

Valtina nodded in reply. "Ladaya warned me this would be a difficult mission. I need to see if I can enter Rachel's mind. That will give us an idea of what we're up against."

"I'll join you," Demetri offered. "If the fury senses your presence, you'll need backup."

"I will wait here," Fatima stated plainly. "When you return, we'll visit Sean. I will be of more help with the demon."

Valtina and Demetri nodded, and then glided through the apartment to Rachel's bedroom. The noises issuing from the room made it clear that its inhabitants were indeed engaged in animalistic sexual behavior. "Wait here, outside the door," Valtina instructed Demetri. She was uncomfortable with the idea of watching Rachel and her partner; sharing the experience with Demetri would only make it worse. The warrior seemed to sense Valtina's anxiety, and agreed to remain outside.

"I'll know if you need me," he promised Valtina as she entered the bedroom.

Valtina was overwhelmed by what she found beyond the door. The room resembled a torture dungeon more than a bedroom. Rachel was tied to a Saint Andrew's cross with leather straps. Her partner was spanking her with a large cat-o-nine tail while she begged him to punish her harder. Valtina was repulsed; the scene before her was the exact opposite of love. She was relieved to find she was able to enter Rachel's mind, but utterly discouraged by what she found there.

Neither Rachel nor the fury seemed to sense Valtina's presence. She was able to examine their thoughts, which were intricately and tightly woven together. Valtina was able to hear the thoughts, but unable to insert inspiration in Rachel's mind. She left the room, and returned to Fatima with Demetri.

"Ladaya was right; I can't exert influence over Rachel as long as the fury possesses her. I'm afraid that repairing Rachel once the fury is expelled is going to be challenging. She's been under the influence of the monster for so long, she's taken on some of its traits.

Rachel is enjoying what's going on in there just as much as the fury is. I don't know how she'll react to what she's done once she's in control again."

"I can repair her, no matter the damage," Fatima said softly. "If there's nothing you can do for her now, we best move on to Sean. I know how to find him." Fatima took Valtina and Demetri by the hands and turned on the spot. Immediately, the trio was transported to the parking lot of an apartment building.

Chapter Three

"There's only one demon, but he has a hound with him," Fatima observed, staring off to the east side of the building. Her powers allowed her to assess the situation from afar.

"Ladaya said we should observe their shift schedule," Valtina told the others. "Perhaps I can enter the demon's mind, see how long he expects to be here. I'll be right back." Valtina disappeared in a flash before Demetri or Fatima could protest. Demetri set off after her, but found he wasn't needed. The demon hadn't sensed Valtina any more than the fury had. Demetri followed again as Valtina returned to Fatima.

"He's due to leave in one hour," she reported. "I think it would be best to overcome him, and move Sean before the next shift arrives."

"But how, Valtina?" Fatima asked softly. "We can't risk confronting him inside the building. There are too many innocents around… they could get injured or even killed if they get in the way."

"I've read his mind, and I know his weakness," Valtina explained. "He's quite full of lust, and he's resentful of being put on guard duty. He thinks it's beneath him. I'll show myself, and I'll seduce him…

convince him I'm on his side… we know that there are scorned spirits working for Morgonda. I'll pretend I'm one of them. I'll draw him out… you two can catch him off guard, and get rid of him and the hellhound safely."

"It's a dangerous plan Valtina," Demetri argued. "If he senses for one minute that you're lying to him, we could all be in danger."

"We ARE all in danger," Fatima reminded him. "We must do what has to be done. Valtina, I can help you convince the demon. In fact," she paused and waved her hand over Valtina, "you can now pass as a demon yourself. Don't worry, I'll set you right as soon as this is over," she assured Valtina, who was panicked by the fire burning behind her eyes. She knew that she now had the red eyes of a demon.

Resolved to her task, Valtina glided through the apartment building, and found Sean's demon guard still standing outside the apartment door. She sauntered up to him, harnessing all of the sexual power within her. The demon startled when he saw her.

"You're new," he growled in surprise. "And you're early."

"Oh, I'm not your relief," Valtina purred, "not your guard relief, anyway. I'd be happy to relieve you in other ways though," she stated coyly. The demon smiled at her devilishly and looked her up and down.

"Well, I'd definitely be interested in that," he smiled. "But I'm on guard duty for another hour."

"Can't you just leave for a little while?" Valtina replied, shifting her cleavage in the demon's face. "Surely a job like this is beneath a powerful spirit like you… I mean, do they really think that this insignificant human warrants around-the-clock surveillance? What's the harm in taking a short break?" she asked mischievously.

The demon smiled. "You're right. This job is a waste of my time. I have my orders… but that's not to say we couldn't go somewhere a bit more private. I can guard him from the parking lot, right? We can use a car close to the main entrance." He took Valtina by the arm and guided her roughly to the parking lot, the hellhound lumbering behind them. Valtina was relieved that the demon had taken her bait; she only hoped that Demetri and Fatima's jobs would be so easy.

The hellhound seemed to sense the presence of the warrior and the child-spirit, and growled when they approached the area where Demetri and Fatima stood invisible.

"What is it buddy? What do you see?" the demon asked in alarm. As he looked down at his dog, Valtina's partners revealed themselves.

"He sees us," Fatima responded firmly, with much more force than Valtina had expected to hear from the pure spirit. Caught off guard, the demon turned just in time to be pierced through the chest by the long silver dagger in Fatima's hand. As the demon disintegrated before Valtina's eyes, Demetri slaughtered the hellhound with his own dagger. "Why am I the only one without a weapon?" Valtina thought again in frustration. She quickly pushed the thought from her mind. She'd promised Ladaya to leave it alone, and there were more important matters at hand.

"We have to move Sean before the next guard gets here," Valtina said urgently. She turned to Fatima. "We need to take him to Rachel. Do you know where she is?"

The emere nodded. "She's having drinks with friends, at the bar across from her apartment."

"Great," Valtina replied, "you two go and stand watch over her. Demetri, you can find me if she moves, right?" Demetri nodded. "I'll inspire Sean to visit the bar. I'm sure there's something in here that will help," she added as she searched her leather satchel. Once again, the magical bag provided exactly what she needed. Valtina nodded goodbye to the others, and then traveled quickly to Sean's apartment.

Before entering, Valtina placed a door-hanger ad for the bar on Sean's outer knob. She found the man sitting quietly in his living room, reading a book. She entered his head, and encouraged him to go out for the evening. Thinking that it was his own idea, Sean rose and collected his wallet and keys. "Perfect!" he thought as he left the apartment and found the ad on his door. "Two-for-one drinks and karaoke. That sounds just perfect."

Valtina rode with Sean as he drove to the bar, but entered ahead of him when they arrived. She found

Fatima and Demetri standing guard near Rachel and her group of friends.

"Do either of you know how much contact they have to have to expel the fury?" Valtina asked breathlessly. "I don't know what kind of shape Rachel will be in once she's freed," she reminded them. "This may not be the time for them to meet."

Fatima nodded. "Sean's presence alone will be enough to rid Rachel of the fury. Once she's gone, you take Rachel away and we'll watch Sean. I'll send Demetri if he leaves before you and Rachel return," Fatima instructed. As the emere spoke, the door of the bar opened and Sean entered. The trio watched as a smoky, opaque being separated from Rachel. The fury spotted Valtina and her companions instantly, and attacked. She flew at Fatima, assuming falsely that the smallest spirit would be the least powerful. Fatima extended one arm, and the fury froze in the air. Demetri reacted instinctively, destroying the fury as quickly as he'd killed the hellhound. Valtina's relief over the destruction of the fury was short lived. The moment after the fury died her backup arrived, in the form of half a dozen wraiths. Dread filled Valtina's heart, but Fatima interrupted her thoughts.

"Valtina, you must take Rachel and leave *now*," Fatima instructed. "Demetri and I can handle them," she said as she brandished her dagger at the approaching monsters, "you must complete the job we were sent here to do. *Go now!*"

Valtina obeyed by entering Rachel's mind. "I think I'd like to go home now," Rachel thought. Valtina guided her out of the bar and back to her apartment across the street. It wasn't until they were safely inside that Valtina read Rachel's thoughts. What she found was an immensely complicated blend of shame and confusion.

"It's alright," Valtina inspired in the woman's thoughts, "I was experimenting. Everyone experiments. And it's okay that I don't want to do it anymore." Valtina removed the shame and confusion from Rachel's mind, and allowed her to rid her bedroom of the evidence of the fury's influence. Valtina felt a slight tug of hesitation before Rachel threw out her vibrator collection. She encouraged her to toss the toys; they were a reminder of what Rachel needed to forget. Valtina made a mental note to replace the collection with toys from the satchel. Once the bedroom had been returned to its original state, Rachel sat for a moment to reflect on her future. She felt different, though she didn't know how or why. Now that she no longer had depraved urges, how would she spend her time? Who would she spend her time with? "There's more out there," Valtina encouraged her. Rachel sat up straight and her mood brightened. "Love is the whole point of life, isn't it?" Rachel asked herself silently, surprised that the word had entered her head. She couldn't remember the last time she'd thought of love. "It's out there," Rachel thought. "It's out there for me. I just have to find it."

With new resolve, Rachel stood and set off for her bedroom to change clothes. She'd suddenly become uncomfortable in her tight, revealing mini-dress. As Rachel changed into a pair of slacks and a sweater set that were pieces of her work wardrobe, Valtina returned to the bar to see how her friends had faired against the wraiths. She found Demetri alone, standing guard over Sean.

"It's alright, Fatima's okay. She returned to The Afterlife to report the wraith attack to the Generals. The fury didn't send for them, Valtina. They were after you. Morgonda knows about you now… we must have a spy in our ranks… though how she found out about you doesn't really matter. She knows about your powers, and she's determined to destroy you. We must finish this mission, but this may be your last. Fatima is alerting the Generals that you've been marked. It may be too dangerous to send you out again."

"I don't care if I'm marked," Valtina said with a surge of determination. "Ladaya said I'm the best chance of destroying the evil armies, and I'm going to continue to fight. I'll be back shortly with Rachel," Valtina finished abruptly and returned to Rachel's apartment. She was overwhelmed by Demetri's news. Valtina had never imagined that her powers were significant enough to draw Morgonda's attention. She understood now why Ladaya was so insistent on protecting her, and now she wanted her own dagger even more. Why shouldn't she be allowed to protect herself? Why were others required to risk themselves for her? With frustration, Valtina entered Rachel's bedroom. She was determined to finish her mission as quickly as possible; she was eager to return to Middle

World and discuss the new developments with Ladaya. Quickly, she entered Rachel's mind.

"Yes, back to the bar. That sounds like a fine idea," Rachel thought as she moved toward her door. Valtina let the woman return ahead of her. Once Rachel had left the hallway, Valtina reached into her leather satchel and retrieved a large box wrapped in plain brown paper. When Rachel returns home, she will find the new toys and assume that she'd ordered them and then forgot about it. Satisfied with her plan, Valtina followed Rachel across the street.

Rachel spotted Sean the moment she entered the bar. She found herself inexplicably drawn to him, and a strange, unfamiliar flutter surged through her chest. Sean turned on his barstool, his eyes locking with Rachel's. Valtina joined Demetri at the seemingly empty table behind Sean.

As Valtina watched the couple, she became more and more aware that the mission would be much easier from then on. True love was working its own magic on the couple, who were finally united after so many years of being forced apart. Rachel and Sean talked passionately, and found that they had many things in common.

"I can't explain this feeling," Rachel began hesitantly, "but it seems like I've known you my whole life." She blushed and immediately felt embarrassed by her confession. "I'm sorry, I'm sure that sounds crazy."

Sean smiled brightly. "Normally, that would sound crazy, but I feel the exact same way. You know, I've never been to this bar before. I hardly ever go out. But earlier this evening I was overwhelmed with the urge to get out and have a few drinks. And now here you are," he said, smiling. "It's almost as if destiny brought us together."

Valtina and Demetri smiled at Sean's statement. Valtina entered the couple's minds in turn, and found that both were overcome with love and affection. The bond between them was solid and unshakable. For a moment, Valtina expected the mist to arrive and take them back to Middle World. When it didn't appear, she sat back and watched Rachel and Sean interact with each other.

"I can't believe I'm about to suggest this," Rachel began, "but I live right across the street. Would you like to go back to my apartment and get to know each other better?" she asked suggestively. Sean readily agreed; he paid their tabs and then followed Rachel to her apartment, with Valtina and Demetri trailing close behind.

Rachel found the box outside of her front door, and immediately recognized the packaging. "Of course!" she found herself thinking. "The backordered toys must have finally arrived." Rachel took the box and led Sean to her bedroom. Demetri hesitated at the bedroom door.

"This is more your area of expertise," he said to Valtina. "I'll stay here, in the hallway, and let you do your work." Valtina nodded in understanding, though she still wasn't sure why she was needed. Rachel and Sean were getting along just fine without any inspiration from her. But since the mist hadn't arrived, Valtina assumed that she still had work to do. She followed the couple inside just as Rachel shut the bedroom door.

Rachel and Sean embraced and kissed each other with a desperate hunger. Sean wrapped Rachel in his arms and guided her to the bed, where they collapsed in a tangle of limbs. He pulled away for a moment and stared into Rachel's eyes.

"I don't want you to think this is something I do on a regular basis," he said sheepishly. "I'm just overwhelmed with the feeling that this is right… that this is where I'm supposed to be, where we both belong."

Valtina felt Rachel twinge with guilt at Sean's words, as thoughts of her past misdeeds filled her head. Valtina removed the guilt from Rachel's heart and the memories of what she'd done under the fury's influence on her mind.

"I understand," Rachel breathed heavily. "I feel the same way. I need you… I can't explain how I know that, I just do." Sean leaned over and nibbled on Rachel's lips. He pulled away again, and this time slowly undressed her, kissing her soft skin as he exposed her body. When she was naked, he backed away and stripped off his own clothing. They remained still for a minute, taking in each other's bodies. Sean smiled and approached Rachel, laying her flat on the bed. He moved over her, once again finding her mouth with his. Rachel reached down and stroked his growing erection as they kissed.

Sean groaned at the touch of Rachel's hand. A fiery excitement he'd never felt before filled his body. "Slow down," he warned her, "I want this to last all night." Rachel slowed the movements of her hand and loosened her grip. Sean moved against her, rubbing his stiff cock against her belly. With one hand, he reached down to explore her pussy. Her wetness was intoxicating, and he quickly moved down to replace his fingers with his mouth. Rachel moved and bucked against him as he thrashed his tongue into her pussy. With one thumb, Sean traced circles around her clit, massaging her to a powerful, body shuddering climax. He drank every drop of juice that flowed from her pussy before pulling her close and kissing her passionately, sharing the taste of her explosion. Rachel sighed in ecstasy, and then remembered the cardboard box.

"Do you want to get a little naughty?" Rachel asked sweetly as she reached for the box.

"What do you have in mind?" he asked eagerly. Rachel opened the package and pulled out a sleek glass dildo.

"Well, we could probably find interesting things to do with this." Valtina quickly searched her satchel and retrieved a bottle of lube; she placed it on the bedside table. Almost immediately, Sean spotted the bottle and grabbed it, and then took the dildo from Rachel.

"This is smaller than my cock," he observed as he lubed up the toy, "maybe I should warm you up with this. Would you like that?" he asked her innocently.

"Oh yes baby," Rachel cried as Sean reached down to tease her with his hand, "give it to me. Please give it to me."

Sean obliged, driving the dildo deep inside Rachel in one swift thrust. Rachel cried out again with pleasure as she squeezed against the toy inside her. Sean teased her with smooth, long strokes as he teased Rachel's nipples with his mouth. Rachel tried to reposition herself.

"You've already made me come once, and now you're about to do it again," she said through heavy breaths. "I think you deserve a little pleasure."

Sean resisted, and moved Rachel back to her original position. "There will be time for that," he sighed. "We have a lifetime, I think, to pleasure each other. I want tonight to be all about you." He increased the speed of his hand, plunging the dildo in and out of Rachel with determination. "I want to see how many times I can make you come tonight," he confessed. The combination of Sean's words and his touch overwhelmed Rachel, and launched her into her second powerful orgasm.

"That makes two." Sean smiled as Rachel caught her breath. She grabbed a bottle of water Valtina had discreetly placed on the nightstand. She gulped down the liquid before turning back to Sean and taking his cock in her hand. She leaned in, nuzzling his neck and then leaving a trail of soft kisses to his earlobe.

"Can I have this now, please?" she begged slightly. "I feel like I've been waiting for this my whole life. Please… please give it to me," she said again.

Sean once again embraced Rachel and laid her on her back. He pushed her legs up and out, leaving her pussy open and completely exposed. He understood what Rachel had said; he felt as if his entire life had been leading him to this moment. Full of exhilaration, he eased his thick, throbbing cock into Rachel's wet, welcoming pussy. The couple gasped in unison at the feeling of finally being connected.

Valtina looked on, a bittersweet feeling filling her heart. She remembered what it felt like to physically connect with her soul-mate; she longed for the end of the war, when she could finally see him again. Valtina scolded herself for letting her mind wander; this was exactly what had gotten her in trouble on her last assignment. She turned her attention back to Sean and Rachel.

The couple continued to move together with slow, passionate motions. Rachel squeezed against Sean's cock, just as she'd done to the dildo. The increased tightness was almost more than Sean could bare, and he felt himself quickly climbing towards his own release. Just as he was about to let himself go and fill Rachel with his climax, she gave him a reason not to.

"If you… can… make me come again," she whispered between breaths, "like… this… I'll let you…

in my ass," she finished, barely able to put words together as Sean increased the speed and vigor of his thrusts. Her offer had excited him, and made him determined to feel her hot juices flow over his member. He quickly pulled out of Rachel and flipped her onto her belly. He pulled her hips towards himself and entered her again; her sharp gasp told Sean that he'd found her G-Spot. He changed his rhythm, thrusting into the spot, pulling just a half-inch away, and then thrusting into it again. Rachel lost all control of her body, and moved against him with animal instinct as he sent her into her third orgasm of the night. He pulled out quickly to avoid finishing with her.

"A promise is a promise," Rachel said sweetly after a few moments of silence. She reached for the bottle of lube. She repositioned herself on all fours, but Sean had other ideas.

"I want to see your face," he explained as he settled her on her back. He placed a pillow under her hips and lubed her forbidden entrance. He teased Rachel's ass with his hand for a moment, exploring her tenderly with his fingers. With one hand he spread Rachel's cheeks wide; with the other he guided the tip of his cock into her. The look on Rachel's face told him she enjoyed the penetration, and he pushed further in.

It was then that Sean noticed the cardboard box still sitting on the edge of the bed. He reached blindly into the box and pulled out a large rabbit vibrator. Rachel met his eyes and smiled; she nodded in agreement to the idea behind Sean's smile. She took the vibrator from him, turned it to full power, and plunged it into her throbbing pussy. The slender rabbit ears enveloped her clit while the shaft of the toy spun inside her; Sean continued sliding his cock gently in and out of her ass, spurred on by the intense vibrations radiating from Rachel's pussy. Just as Rachel thought there were no more sensations to feel, Sean reached down and pinched each of her nipples between his fingers. This final rush of electricity sent Rachel over the edge again, and she growled fiercely as she exploded in the most powerful orgasm she'd ever had. She felt more sure now than ever that Sean was exactly who she belonged with.

Rachel's orgasm triggered Sean's, and with a final thrust he emptied his juices into Rachel's ass. He slid out of her and crawled to the head of the bed; he laid Rachel's head on his chest and leaned back on the headboard.

"Do you feel that?" he asked her as his heart beat against her hand. "That's yours. My heart and every other part of me belong to you." Tears filled Rachel's eyes as she bathed in a happiness she'd never dreamed of. As she lifted her head to respond, the mist appeared and carried Valtina home.

Chapter Four

When the mist cleared, Valtina was certain she'd been delivered to the wrong place. A thick layer of grey fog filled the air, making it impossible for Valtina to see anything in front of her. She heard a slight pop, and turned to find Demetri standing only inches behind her.

"This can't be good," he stated grimly, gesturing to the fog. "Didn't anyone meet you?" he asked with confusion.

"No, but I've only just arrived. You must have been right behind me. What do you think could be causing this?" she asked in fear.

"Think about it Valtina… has Ladaya told you about the black fog spreading on Earth?"

"Yes… but you don't think…" Valtina's voice cracked as she realized the worst had happened.

"I'm afraid Demetri's right," Ladaya's voice traveled through the fog. The returning spirits heard their General before they saw her. "Middle World has been breached." She sighed desperately, finally appearing a few feet before them. "We have no proof, but with Morgonda learning about you and our sanctuary compromised, I think it's safe to say that there is a traitor in our midst," Ladaya said with frustration and despair.

"Middle World is no longer safe," she continued. "From this moment on, you two are to stick together. Don't leave each other's sight for a moment. I think it would be best if you left on your next mission as soon as possible. I must consult with my superior, and determine where you're most needed. I'll return as quickly as possible." Ladaya disappeared, leaving no time for Valtina or Demetri to respond.

Valtina was filled with disappointment. She was happy that Ladaya intended to let her continue her assignments, even though she had a price on her head. But she'd been hoping for a chance to talk with Ladaya; there were questions she needed answered.

"I guess we're stuck with each other for now," Demetri said, smiling sadly.

"Demetri, do you know what will happen if we lose?" The question had been nagging at Valtina since the moment she saw the grey fog. If they could infiltrate Middle World, what else was the enemy capable of?

Demetri sighed. "If we lose, we will no longer exist. There will be no distinction between the Underworld, Earth, Middle World, or The Afterlife. Everywhere will be filled with monsters."

"We won't let that happen," Valtina said firmly, with determination.

"No," Demetri agreed, "no we won't."

And with that, the weary spirit soldiers settled under the willow tree and waited patiently for their General to return.

-*To be continued in Book 6-*

If you enjoyed this title, I would appreciate your leaving a review of the book. Good reviews encourage an author to write as well as help books to sell. Good reviews can be just a few short sentences describing what you liked about the book without having a spoiler. If you could spend 30 seconds writing a review, I would appreciate it: you can review this title right now at your favorite retailer.

Here is a preview of the **next story** you may enjoy:

True Lovers - The Leather Satchel Romance Series, Book 6

VALTINA AND Demetri sat silently under the willow tree, anxiously awaiting Ladaya's return. They'd stopped trying to guess how much time had passed since Ladaya returned to The Afterlife; they were now marking the time by the number of wraiths Demetri had slaughtered. So far, the warrior had eliminated five of the monsters. Valtina had known that their sanctuary had been breached, but it hadn't seemed real until she saw the first black hooded creature emerge from the dense grey fog. As time passed, Valtina became more and more nervous; she knew that in this situation, no news was not good news.

Demetri stiffened, and Valtina followed his gaze. Another wraith was approaching from the fog. As the warrior rose to confront the monster, the tip of a silver dagger broke through its chest, and it evaporated where it stood. Ladaya and a spirit Valtina didn't recognize stood before them.

"Ladaya!" Valtina exclaimed, "I was starting to worry!"

"Hello, August." Demetri nodded to the other spirit. August nodded in reply. Demetri continued. "Valtina, this is August, my General. I take it no one is traveling alone now?" he asked, turning to the Generals.

"It's nice to meet you, Valtina. I've heard wonderful things," August began. He turned to Demetri. "No, we've all been instructed to travel with a partner. The wraiths are flooding Middle World, and we believe they're looking for a way in to The Afterlife."

Ladaya watched panic spread over Valtina's face. "Don't worry child," she assured her. "We've learned of a way to defeat them. There's lore of a weapon, a sword forged in the fires of the Underworld that will destroy the wraith army. If the Queen is decapitated with the sword, the entire army will evaporate. They're all connected, you see…" Ladaya trailed off.

"Are we sure the weapon exists?" Demetri asked with an air of doubt. "I mean, lore isn't always reliable."

"We're pretty confident," August answered. "The rest of the lore regarding wraiths has proved true. We have no reason to think the sword is any different."

"So, do you know where it is?" Valtina asked. "Let us help, we can search with the other spirits."

Ladaya smiled. "Once again, I appreciate your offer, and your dedication… but we all have specific jobs to do, and your next mission is the most important to date. Other spirits, whose gifts are suited to the mission, are searching for the sword."

"Ladaya, speaking of weapons…" Valtina began, but was interrupted by her General.

"I know, Valtina," Ladaya sighed. "You want a weapon. As well you should, knowing that Morgonda is targeting you. And at this point, I'd give you a dagger if

I could. But I don't believe it would do you much good."

"Why not?" Valtina asked.

"Demetri," Ladaya turned to the warrior, "would you be so kind as to let Valtina hold your dagger for a moment?"

Nodding in confusion, Demetri held his dagger out to Valtina. The moment she touched the weapon, her hand burned in pain. Gasping, she pulled away.

"Ouch!" she cried. "I can't even touch it?!"

"No," Ladaya sighed, "Valtina, your spirit is composed of pure love. The weapon, and its purpose, is in direct conflict with your spirit force, making it impossible for you to hold it."

Valtina was disappointed; she also wished Ladaya had told her that the first time she'd asked for a weapon. It would have saved her a lot of frustration. But the fog continued to grow denser, and Valtina knew that she must stay focused on her mission. "Ok, so I can't protect myself. Where are we going next?" she asked with a slight tone of defeat.

"Las Vegas," Ladaya answered. "We've learned of a dire situation there. I'm sending you to a young woman named Penelope. Her father was a non-denominational minister who worked to help the souls of Sin City. Six years ago, the preacher made a drastic change in his ministry and began preaching vehemently against 'sins of the flesh'. He brainwashed his congregation to believe that even marital sex can bring evil into the home, and should only be indulged in for the purpose of procreation. The result of these ministries has been a sharp decrease in the number of soul-mates pairing up. They believe that their natural sexual attraction goes against God, and that the person they belong with is the person they are LEAST physically attracted to."

If you enjoyed this sample then look for **True Lovers - The Leather Satchel Romance Series, Book 6.**

Here is a preview of **another story** you may enjoy:

Exposed - The Daemon Paranormal Romance Chronicles, Book 5

IN PERU, Supay and Phoebe had just welcomed their daughter into the world. The tiny infant was named Irene. To the outside world, the little family seemed like a nexus of harmony. Few outsiders would realize the number of troubles they had gone through in the last few years.

It had all started when Phoebe was approached by Apollo. Raised in foster care, she never knew that she was a daemon. Until that day, Phoebe had made all of her money by telling fortunes. As a daemon, she had a unique talent—her ability was to read people's minds and see what their innermost thoughts were. When Apollo showed up, he needed help finding the Qilin. According to the prophecy, the Qilin would indicate the next great leader or wise man. Apollo had drawn her into the hunt because the Qilin was going under a different name, and he needed someone to read minds in order to find her. Together, they had quickly located the Qilin and started a passionate romance. Before long, it ended. Phoebe discovered at the death of the Qilin that Apollo's talent was to give suggestions or manipulate the minds of other people. Due to this, Phoebe could never truly trust him. She could not be certain that her love for him was not just another manipulation. At the same time, she discovered that her dog was actually a shape shifter known as Supay. Although she had felt betrayed at first, she came to terms with this oddity over time. Supay had become her dog so that he could protect her and hopefully save the

Qilin. Although it had not helped the Qilin, his protection had kept her safe.

Phoebe picked up Irene and sat down in the rocking chair. It was so peaceful in the nursery. Before long, Supay would return home. Although the infighting among the daemons had died down, it still caused problems. Supay had been stretched to the maximum of his abilities as he tried to bring peace. Their desire to bring peace had come at a temporary cost; the meddlesome siren, Juno, had agreed to stop causing arguments and fighting among the daemons, provided Phoebe give up her memories. Although Phoebe eventually got those memories back, it had led to a temporary break from Juno.

As Irene fell asleep, Phoebe walked into the living room. She started to sit down when Supay walked in. He immediately came up to her for a kiss.

"How are my lovely ladies today?" he asked. Phoebe held him closer and kissed him back hungrily.

"The little one is fine, but the older one needs some attention," she teased. Supay held her closer. Her scent was enticing. Everywhere he turned in his apartment, he could smell her. Running his fingers through her hair, he pulled her head back for another kiss. The ferocity of her passion surprised him and made him want more. Setting his things down, he looked at her inquisitively. Slowly, he started to unbutton his jacket and waited for her to respond. When she started to pull off her shirt as well, he was certain. She wanted him.

Quietly, they slipped off their clothes and sank to the floor. Like secret trysts among teenagers, they had to remain quiet and not wake up Irene. Running his finger down her naked body, Supay started to play with her clit. He slipped his fingers inside of her and realized how wet she was.

"Mmm... you know, we could try putting that jade necklace on again," he teased. Reaching onto the table, he wrapped the necklace around her neck. Given to her by the Qilin, it was the only reason she could even have children with him. Without the aid of the fertility talisman, she would never have been able to have children outside of her daemon family.

If you enjoyed this sample then look for **Exposed - The Daemon Paranormal Romance Chronicles, Book 5**.

Other Books by Darla Dunbar

- The Romeo Alpha BBW Paranormal Shifter Romance Series

- Romeo Alpha Blood Lines Romance Series

- The Alpha Feud BBW Paranormal Shifter Romance Series

- The Alpha Packed BBW Paranormal Shifter Romance Series

- The Daemon Paranormal Romance Chronicles

- The Mind Talker Paranormal Romance Series

Get the latest update on new releases from the author at:

https://darladunbar.com/newsletter/

About the Author - Darla Dunbar

Darla has been interested in paranormal romance since she was a teenager in high school. It was then that she discovered she could fulfill her fantasies through her writing.

Observing people and human behavior in the area of romance has always been one of her favorite pastimes. Combining that with an overactive imagination is a sure fire way of coming up with interesting themes.

Connect with Darla Dunbar

I really appreciate you reading my book! Here are my social media coordinates:

Friend me on Facebook: https://www.facebook.com/darladunbar/

Follow me on Twitter: https://twitter.com/DarlDunbar

Check me out on Goodreads: https://www.goodreads.com/author/show/8425857.Darl a_Dunbar

Subscribe to my newsletter: https://darladunbar.com/newsletter/

Visit my website: https://darladunbar.com/